HONEY, I
BLEW UP
THE KID

HONEY, I BLEW UP THE KID

A Novel by Todd Strasser
Based on the Motion Picture from Walt Disney Pictures
Co-Producer Dennis E. Jones
Executive Producers Albert Band and Stuart Gordon
Based on Characters Created by Stuart Gordon & Brian Yuzna
& Ed Naha
Based on the Screenplay by Thom Eberhardt and Peter Elbling
& Garry Goodrow and Story by Garry Goodrow
Produced by Dawn Steel and Edward S. Feldman
Directed by Randal Kleiser

SCHOLASTIC INC.
New York Toronto London Auckland Sydney

ISBN 0-590-46396-9

Text and illustrations copyright © 1992 by The Walt Disney Company. All rights reserved. Published by Scholastic Inc., 730 Broadway, New York, NY 10003, by arrangement with Disney Press.

12 11 10 9 8 7 6 5 4 3 2 1   2 3 4 5 6 7/9

Printed in the U.S.A.   40

First Scholastic printing, September 1992

HONEY, I BLEW UP THE KID

CHAPTER

It was a perfectly normal day for the Szalinskis.

Whirr, whirr, click, buzz. Wayne Szalinski's shaving invention was working smoothly. It sat on his head like a hat and was strapped under his chin. The mirror in front rotated with an electric motor whenever he needed to see another part of his face. It had everything he thought he might need hanging from it. He called it the Magi-Shave. When Wayne was using the Magi-Shave, he could even walk around the house while he got ready for work.

"Oomph!"

The problem was that he just couldn't see where he was going. Also, every time he moved his head to the right, he got hit with the shaving cream that hung from the right-hand side of the mirror. The Magi-Shave was a good idea that needed more work. It was that way with a lot of Wayne's inventions.

Down the hall, fourteen-year-old Nick Szalinski was

in his room, strumming an electric guitar and thinking about a girl. The guitar made some very strange noises, but Nick hardly noticed. He was in love, and her name was Mandy Park.

In the kitchen, nineteen-year-old Amy was in the middle of an argument with her mother, Diane. Amy was about to go off to college, and Diane wanted to go along to help her get settled. Amy, on the other hand, thought she could handle things by herself. Diane argued with Amy while she made breakfast. She turned on the automatic juice squeezer that Wayne had invented. It kept jamming oranges into the glasses and pushing the glasses onto the floor.

The family dog, Quark, was in the kitchen, too. He'd gotten the mail and had it in his mouth. All he wanted was to have someone take it from him. Nobody noticed.

Upstairs, two-year-old Adam was in his playpen in his room. It was a huge rope cage his father had invented, filled with all of Adam's favorite playthings, including his favorite stuffed animal, Big Bunny. The playpen was also equipped with a television screen and a computer. Adults thought this invention was very clever, but to Adam, it was still a playpen. And Adam wanted to be out of it. He made a face.

In the playpen, a screen flashed a picture of a cat, and a voice said, "See the cat! Can you say *cat?*"

Adam couldn't say *cat.* He could blow a raspberry,

though. He did that to the picture of the cat. That made a rattle shake and some bells ring.

Diane called upstairs to Wayne from the kitchen. "Where's the baby?" she asked.

"He's in the playpen," Wayne called back.

"He gets out of the playpen," Diane said.

"I fixed the playpen," Wayne yelled back to Diane.

"You fixed it before and he got out," Diane said.

Wayne didn't like to be reminded of that, but he knew Diane was right. He walked into Adam's room. Adam was still in the playpen. Even though he knew Diane was right to be concerned, Wayne was a little annoyed that she didn't trust him to fix his own invention. In fact, Wayne was often a little annoyed these days.

The family had just moved from California to Nevada. A company in Nevada called Sterling Laboratories had bought Wayne's big invention. It was a machine that could shrink things. Now, Sterling Labs wanted to redesign the machine so that it would make things bigger. They had hired Wayne to do the work, but it wasn't going well. For some reason, the machine just didn't blow things up as well as it shrank them. Every time another experiment failed—and each one did—Wayne's codirector, Dr. Hendrickson, got angry at Wayne. When things didn't go well, Wayne would sometimes take it out on his family. He didn't expect Dr. Hendrickson to trust him, but he thought at least his own wife should!

"He won't get out this time," Wayne snapped at Diane. Then he talked to Adam. "Will you, big buddy?" he said. "I mean, your daddy can certainly fix a playpen that will hold you. After all, you're just a baby." Adam blew another raspberry.

Wayne went back to the bathroom. He had to finish shaving and put bandages on the cuts he'd given himself. He couldn't watch Adam any longer. Besides, Adam was safe in the playpen.

This was just the opportunity Adam had been waiting for. When he was sure he was alone, Adam worked on the playpen for a few seconds and then was free.

"Nick! Breakfast!" Diane yelled to Adam's big brother.

Nick could barely hear his mother over the noise he was making with his guitar. He could, however, smell the bacon. Besides, there was something he wanted to ask his mother—just *had* to ask her. He turned off his guitar and headed downstairs. Nick was in such a hurry that he paid no attention to Adam. He just stepped right over him. Adam was crawling along the upstairs hallway toward Nick's room.

In the kitchen, Diane finished her argument with Amy. "Amy, it's decided. I'm going with you."

"Mom!" Amy said. She was exasperated. She put both her hands on her hips and glared at her mother. Her mother glared back.

"I don't need your help, Mom. I'm going to California State. It's only a few miles from our old house!"

"I'm going with you, period!" Diane said. Amy stormed out of the kitchen.

Nick didn't hear his mother and sister arguing. He was thinking about Mandy. Mandy was very pretty, but she hadn't seemed to notice that Nick was alive. He thought he needed some advice.

"Mom," he said. "Let's say you were a girl . . ."

"I think I can visualize it," Diane said.

"Would you think I was a nerd?" Nick asked. "Just looking at me, I mean?"

Diane had an idea now of what was on Nick's mind. "Any particular girl?" she asked.

Nick tried to look very casual, as if he didn't have anybody specific in mind. He didn't want his mother to know he had a crush.

"No," he said. "Just a girl, any old girl, I might, you know, want to ask to go to the movies or something. You know?"

She knew. "Take it from me, kiddo. You're turning into a very handsome young man. You're going to be just like your father."

At that moment, Wayne walked into the kitchen. His Magi-Shave was going wild. The mirror bounced up and down. Mouthwash splattered on the floor. Shaving cream dripped from Wayne's cheeks.

Nick took one look at him, groaned, and ran up to his room.

CHAPTER 2

Whirr, whirr, click, boing! The Magi-Shave wouldn't stop.

Quark dropped the mail and ran for safety.

Diane was used to this kind of thing. Without batting an eye, she walked behind Wayne and tried to find the on/off switch at the back of the helmet. It was stuck. She spoke as she fiddled with it.

"Now, if you and Nick want to go out by yourselves while I'm in California with Amy, I've got the name of a baby-sitter who can watch Adam."

Wayne noticed then that Nick was gone. "What's wrong with him?" he asked Diane.

"I think there might be a girl," Diane explained.

The motor stopped whining, and the mirror was still. There was quiet for a second until there was a scream. It came from Nick's room. It came from Nick. He couldn't believe what he was looking at. His little baby brother was in the middle of his room, and it

6

was a total mess! Adam had broken the strings of Nick's electric guitar! He had even smeared chocolate on Nick's CD player! Nick wanted to kill Adam.

"Uh-oh," Adam said. He was in trouble and he knew it. Being cute wasn't going to get him out of this!

"Grrrrrr!" said Nick. He was already planning the murder.

Adam crawled toward the door, fast. "Adam go bye-bye," he said.

"You won't just go bye-bye, you're going to go into the next solar system, you little punk!"

That was as much as Adam was going to take. He sat back down and looked defiant. Then he held his nose and made a terrible face to show his brother that he didn't like him *either*.

Nick was about to attack. Diane arrived and stopped him from mutilating Adam. Then Diane turned to Adam and shook her finger at the baby.

"No! No, Adam," she said.

"Saw-wee, Mama. Saw-wee," Adam said. He sounded as if he really meant it, too. Diane picked him up and took him back to the kitchen with her.

Amy looked into Nick's room. She laughed, then said, "Now you know what it's like having a creepy little brother." Nick didn't find that comforting.

Wayne felt bad for Nick. "Oh no," he said when he saw the mess. "I guess the Auto-Tend Playpen needs a little more work."

Nick thought that was an understatement.

CHAPTER 3

Wayne had to take Adam to the day-care center on his way to work, and he had to drop Nick off at his summer job. Diane and Amy had called a taxi to take them to the airport.

"I don't know how he keeps getting out of the playpen," Wayne said to Diane while he put on his sports jacket.

"Maybe you ought to forget the playpen idea," Diane said gently. But Wayne wasn't the kind of man who liked to admit defeat.

"Look, I said I can fix it. I'm not stupid!"

Diane wanted to make Wayne feel better. "I never said you were stupid," she told him. She smiled and put her arms around him. "In fact, you're the smartest guy I know," she said. Then she kissed him.

Then they both smiled and said together, "Which says a lot about the guys you know!"

It was a joke they had shared many times, and it made them laugh and kiss again.

Adam watched and then held his nose. He didn't think much of kissing.

Diane had noticed how easily Wayne got upset these days. She was worried about him. "Wayne, is there anything wrong at work?" she asked.

Wayne didn't want to make Diane worry the way he did. "Well, expanding matter is turning out to be a bit more difficult than shrinking it," he said. That didn't sound very serious.

Diane still thought there was more to the story than that. "But, you're happy? I mean, they're treating you all right?"

"Sure! Everything is fine!" Wayne said. Diane was sure from the way he said it that it wasn't true at all. She was even more worried now. She wanted to talk to Wayne, but just then the taxi arrived to take her and Amy to the airport. She would have to wait until she got back from California to find out what was going on.

Diane and Amy carried their luggage to the taxi. Wayne carried Adam out onto the lawn to say goodbye to them. Wayne wanted Diane to know that he could take care of Adam. Diane wanted Wayne to know that it was a big job to take care of a little kid.

"So, hopefully, they'll tire him out at day care, so when I get home, he can take a late nap—"

"No nap!" Adam shouted.

"We don't say the *N* word around two year olds," Diane reminded him. Then she went on with her other suggestions. "His lunch is in the freezer. The baby-sitter's number is on the refrigerator—"

"Diane, don't you think I can handle things around the house for a few days?"

Wayne wasn't sure he wanted to know the answer to that question, but Diane just answered it by giving him another kiss. Adam squeezed his nose in disgust. Amy sighed. The cab driver honked.

"Break it up, guys," Amy said. "We've got to go."

Wayne looked at his watch. "So do *we*!" he said. He didn't have a minute to spare.

CHAPTER

Wayne dashed along the shiny bare hallway of Sterling Laboratories. He could tell from the voice on the public-address system that the next test was about to begin.

"Szalinski, test number one-two-seven-seven. Crystal. Group five."

One thousand two hundred seventy-seven tests had been conducted already? It seemed impossible that he'd been at this company for less than a year but had already failed that many times.

Inside a large experiment room Dr. Charles Hendrickson was readying things for the test. He was not happy to be working with Wayne Szalinski on this invention. Dr. Hendrickson was the kind of person who thought he himself could never make a mistake, so it had to be Wayne's fault that the machine wasn't working right. And now, Wayne was late again.

Dr. Hendrickson made a face.

"Data recorders to high speed. Time mark," he said into a microphone.

As the lights dimmed, Dr. Hendrickson and all the other scientists in the room put on goggles.

In the middle of the room was a very large machine. It looked like a gigantic microscope, and it was aimed at a blue crystal cube that sat on a nearby pedestal.

There was an electromagnetic buzz, and red lasers began pulsating along the length of the machine. The lasers joined together and then struck the blue crystal. The crystal vibrated. It swelled and expanded. Then it melted into a blob. And, finally, the blob blew up, splattering Dr. Hendrickson with blue gel.

The door to the room flew open. Wayne ran in.

"Sorry, everybody. There were some largish cumulonimbus clouds blocking the sun. . . . Uh, my, uh, van, it's solar, see? It needs sunshine for solar energy in order to run. It's good for the environment. And then I had to drop my son off at day care. . . ."

Dr. Hendrickson just glared at him, then marched out of the room. He signaled the other scientists to follow him. Wayne was left alone with his invention and a lot of globs of messy blue gel. Wayne didn't think that was fair. He ran after Dr. Hendrickson.

Dr. Hendrickson was talking to the other scientists. "Clifford Sterling demands results," he was saying. "So do the stockholders and the U.S. government! And, as project director—"

"Excuse me, Dr. Hendrickson," Wayne began.

Dr. Hendrickson pretended to be polite, but what he said wasn't polite at all. "I beg your pardon, Wayne. But as project *co*director, I intend to deliver results."

"Dr. Hendrickson . . ."

"What is it, Szalinski?"

Wayne pulled some papers out of his briefcase. They fell all over the floor. Wayne tried to pick them up and talk at the same time. Dr. Hendrickson took the opportunity to keep on walking.

"I've been doing some work on my own on the problem," Wayne said, even though it wasn't easy to talk to somebody who was walking away from him.

"Now, Szalinski, when you licensed your device to Sterling Labs, you were promised that the finest minds in the country would be working with you." It was clear that Dr. Hendrickson meant himself.

"Yes, sir, I know that," Wayne said. He had all his papers gathered now. He stood up. His papers fell down again. "I have some notes," he said. "Dr. Hendrickson?"

There was no answer.

Dr. Hendrickson was gone. He and the other scientists had disappeared, leaving Wayne and his notes alone in the hall.

CHAPTER 5

That evening, back at home, Nick spent a lot of time in his room. He had to clean it up. He also wanted to think about what had happened that day at the swimming pool where he worked. Mandy had actually *spoken* to him. Of course, she'd called him Rick, not Nick. And then, just when Nick was about to get up the courage to ask her to a movie, his father had arrived to take him home. Mandy and her friends had thought the solar-powered van was too weird. It was odd looking and had big solar panels attached to the roof and sides. Nick had wanted to disappear into the ground. Instead, he'd climbed in the van.

Maybe tomorrow Mandy would remember his name. Now that was something to think about. Then he smelled something odd. Maybe this wasn't a good time to think. Nick went to investigate.

Down in the kitchen, Wayne was talking to Diane on the telephone. She needed to make sure that she could leave her men alone for a few days without worrying about anything.

"How was your flight?" Wayne asked. He was using a telephone he had invented that fit on his head like a helmet. He could walk around and do things and talk at the same time, which was good, because there were a lot of things to do.

First of all, he had to get rid of the cloud of smoke that was pouring out of the oven. He fanned his arms through it.

Nick arrived with the fire extinguisher.

"Here? Why, everything's great!" Wayne said. Then he pulled open the oven door. More smoke and then flames burst into the kitchen. Nick sprayed the fire extinguisher. The flames disappeared.

"The baby?" Wayne said into the phone. "He's fine. He's in the playpen. . . . No, it's fixed. He can't get out."

Wayne handed Nick a skin diver's face mask and a pair of two-foot-long tongs. Nick put on the face mask to keep smoke out of his eyes and reached into the oven with the tongs.

"So how's Amy's dorm room?" Wayne asked. It wasn't easy to keep his voice calm. Quark was pulling desperately at the leg of his pants. "Stop it, Quark!" he hissed. Quark didn't stop.

On the top of the stove, a pot began to boil over. Wayne couldn't decide whether to clean up the spill with a sponge or turn off the heat or help Nick or see what Quark wanted. He just talked to Diane.

Bubbling liquid oozed down the side of the stove.

Quark barked and tugged.

Nick gagged and coughed while he reached into the oven.

And outside, an ice-cream truck played its music.

Wayne knew that meant trouble. He dashed out of the kitchen. "Uh-huh. Uh-huh. Hmmm," he said to Diane.

He stumbled through the living room, tripping over a footstool that had been pushed over to the front door. He'd feared the worst; he was right. Adam had escaped from his playpen, pushed the footstool to the front door, climbed on it to reach the doorknob, and opened the door. He was outside and headed for trouble. Adam couldn't resist an ice-cream truck. He was all the way down to the sidewalk and almost to the street!

Wayne tugged the phone off his head and dashed after Adam. With every second, Adam was getting closer to the street. Wayne ran faster. Cars and trucks whizzed by. Wayne didn't want to think what might happen *if* . . . Just as Adam reached the end of the sidewalk, Wayne got there, too. He scooped Adam up under one arm and carried him back to the house. He flew in the door, grabbed the telephone, slipped it back on his head, and dashed into the kitchen.

"Really?" he said into the phone, though he had no idea what Diane had just told him. He gasped for breath and sat down at the table. He held Adam firmly on his lap. Nick held up a charred black mass with the tongs and blew out the remaining flames.

"The chicken?" Wayne said, realizing that Diane was asking about their dinner. "Oh, right, the chicken you left for us. Well, it looks mighty good, honey. Nice and crispy."

Quark growled. He knew what *he* was going to have for dinner.

CHAPTER

After dinner—peanut butter sandwiches all around— it was Adam's bedtime. Wayne tucked Adam into his crib, brought the covers up under his chin, and gave him Big Bunny. Wayne hugged Adam, and Adam hugged Big Bunny.

Wayne sat down next to the crib and began singing Adam's favorite song, "Alouette." Adam blinked his eyes and then closed them.

"Je te plumerai les yeux, je te plumerai les yeux."

Wayne had sung the song so many times he didn't even have to think about the words. He looked around the darkened room as he sang. He saw the playpen and the toys. He saw more stuffed animals and crayons and paper. He saw a balloon.

"Et le bec! Et le bec! Et la tête! Et la tête! Al-ouette!..."

Wayne kept looking at the balloon. Then he stopped singing.

He snapped his fingers. "That's it!" he said. "A balloon!"

Dr. Hendrickson was in his office at Sterling Laboratories. It was too late in the day to be doing any experiments, but it wasn't too late for him to be trying to impress people. The person he was trying to impress now was Terence Wheeler. Mr. Wheeler was on the board of directors of Sterling Laboratories. Both Dr. Hendrickson and Mr. Wheeler thought that the company had a great future—*if* Wayne's invention could be made to work properly.

"It'll be a wonderful thing for you, Dr. Hendrickson—if it works."

"I'll make it work," Dr. Hendrickson promised.

"Well, over the years, I've seen Clifford Sterling attach himself to one harebrained idea after another," Mr. Wheeler said. Although he was on the board of directors, he didn't think much of Mr. Sterling, the company's founder. He went on. "I have to tell you, the board is very worried."

Dr. Hendrickson's phone rang. He picked it up. It was the last person he wanted to hear from. It was Wayne Szalinski. Dr. Hendrickson thought Wayne Szalinski was a fool, and he couldn't imagine how Wayne had invented a machine that could change the size of matter. Dr. Hendrickson was sure he'd be making more progress if he didn't have to work with Wayne. Everything Wayne did seemed so silly. It was

19

just a waste of time. He barely listened as Wayne talked.

Suddenly there was a loud popping sound over the telephone. Dr. Hendrickson didn't like loud noises.

"What was *that?*" he asked, annoyed.

"That was the sound of a balloon popping," Wayne said. He was very excited. Dr. Hendrickson wasn't impressed, but Wayne went on. "See, I got this idea while singing my kid to sleep. He had a balloon in his room and it got me thinking. We all know that if you hit a balloon with too much force, you don't allow the molecules enough time to expand, and the balloon pops."

Dr. Hendrickson yawned. Mr. Wheeler wanted to know who was on the phone. Dr. Hendrickson crossed his eyes, which was his way of telling Mr. Wheeler that it was Wayne on the phone.

Mr. Wheeler nodded. Then Dr. Hendrickson covered the phone with his hand and spoke to Mr. Wheeler. "Why Clifford insists on keeping Szalinski involved is beyond me. We'd be neck-deep in apples the size of Buicks by now if I were running this project."

"There are those of us on the board who would agree with you," Mr. Wheeler said. Those were the very words Dr. Hendrickson had been hoping to hear. It meant that there was a good chance he might get a gigantic promotion! He was so excited by what Mr. Wheeler had said that he didn't listen to what Wayne was saying to him over the telephone.

". . . We need to lower the intensity of the electromagnetic pulse to give the molecules time to expand without tearing the atomic fabric."

Dr. Hendrickson had a sudden image of a crane changing the sign outside the building from Sterling Laboratories to Hendrickson Laboratories. He liked that image a lot. All he had to do was make Wayne's invention work.

"Hello? Hello? Are you there?" Wayne asked over the phone.

Dr. Hendrickson had forgotten that Wayne was talking. The man never made any sense anyway, so it wasn't important to listen to him, was it?

"Okay. Why don't you write up this balloon research?" Dr. Hendrickson said. He thought that might keep Wayne busy and out of his hair for a long time. "Oh, and have a good weekend, Szalinski."

Dr. Hendrickson hung up the phone. He didn't want to talk to Wayne anymore. He'd much rather talk to Mr. Wheeler.

Across town, Wayne was wondering if Dr. Hendrickson had heard a word he'd said. He didn't understand Dr. Hendrickson. Wayne was sure he had found the key to the problem with his invention. How could Dr. Hendrickson be so uninterested? Wayne was sick of playing second fiddle to a man who just wanted a promotion. He was sick of being laughed at. He was sick of being blamed for everything that had gone wrong. Wayne was sick of the whole thing, and he was tired of it, too. It was making him cranky. He'd almost gotten into a fight with Diane this morning just because he was upset about work. That wasn't right at all. It was time to change things, to take matters into his own hands.

Wayne had invented his shrinking machine in his own attic in his own house, without any help from lab assistants, project codirectors, or boards of directors. He could now make the machine enlarge matter the same way.

Suddenly Wayne felt good. Tomorrow was Saturday. The lab would be empty. First thing in the morning, he'd get over there and test his new theory on his own—with a little bit of help from Nick. And, of course, they'd bring Adam. Then it would almost be like working in his own attic in his own home. And, Wayne thought, that was the way it should be.

CHAPTER

It was just a few minutes past sunrise the next day when Wayne, Nick, and Adam arrived at Sterling Laboratories.

Adam was in his stroller, wearing his favorite red overalls with the big pocket in front. He clutched Big Bunny and then held the stuffed animal up so it could see everything.

"We need to be a little, uh, discreet about this," Wayne said to Nick. He didn't trust Dr. Hendrickson. He didn't know what to expect, but he knew Dr. Hendrickson wouldn't want him to be there.

"Uh-oh," Adam said. He had spotted the security guard.

"Ah, Mr. Szalinski," the guard said. He was surprised to see anyone at this hour. "Working today?"

"No, Smitty," Wayne answered. "Just in to, uh, tidy up a few things." He didn't tell Smitty that what he wanted to tidy up was everything that had ever gone wrong since he'd come to work at Sterling Laboratories.

The three Szalinskis hurried past the guard and into the laboratory where the machine was kept. They didn't see Smitty pick up the phone and punch in a number.

Wayne flipped switches and turned dials. Soon the whole lab seemed to be alive with flashing lights and buzzing indicators. Adam thought it was a light show just for him and Big Bunny. For the moment, he sat in his stroller and clapped his hands.

Nick was thrilled when his father asked him to help. There were times when Nick wished his father were like everybody else's father. He'd been really embarrassed in the parking lot at work yesterday. But now, that was forgotten. He could barely believe that *his* father, the weird, oddball Wayne Szalinski, was actually in charge of everything in this lab. Wayne had even *invented* it all.

"Wow, this is some lab," Nick said.

"Better than what I used to have in the attic, huh, Nick?"

"Way better," Nick agreed.

Wayne put Nick to work typing commands into the keyboard of a computer console.

"Call up a command directory labeled Primary Laser Drive and tell me what it says under Intensity," said Wayne.

Nick typed. The computer took a few nanoseconds and then flashed a message on the screen.

"It says Access Denied," Nick reported.

"Darn." This was exactly what Wayne was afraid would happen. Dr. Hendrickson was trying to cut him out of the work altogether. But Wayne wasn't going to be stopped like that. After all, he'd invented the machine. He could invent a way to make it work without Dr. Hendrickson's computer.

"Somehow, we've got to cut down the intensity of the lasers," he said. Then he crinkled his eyebrows. That meant he was thinking.

Nick was thinking, too. He picked up an empty soda bottle that had been left on the console. He looked through the thick glass at the bottle's bottom. It gave him an idea. "We could diffuse it with this—maybe," he said. He handed the bottle to his father.

"Great idea!" Wayne said. He took the soda bottle and smashed it against the edge of a table. It shattered into hundreds of pieces. The thick bottom of the bottle looked like a lens. That was just what Wayne needed. He lodged it into a section of the machine labeled Filter Pack.

"Now we're going to set Final Target," Wayne said.

"But what are you going to enlarge, Dad?" Nick asked.

Wayne looked around. He wanted to find something that would be better if it were bigger. He also wanted to show both of his sons that he was a good scientist. He didn't think they'd be impressed if he used a blue crystal like Dr. Hendrickson kept doing. He wanted something special—*very* special.

And what was more special than Big Bunny? That was Adam's favorite toy. He'd love it even more if it were bigger.

"Let me borrow this guy," he said, taking the stuffed animal from Adam. "We're going to make Big Bunny into a much bigger bunny!"

Adam seemed to think that was okay. Wayne put Big Bunny on the target pedestal and started flipping switches again. Nick helped him. They were having fun. They were having so much fun that they didn't notice that Adam was having second thoughts.

"Bunny gone bye-bye," Adam said. That didn't make him happy. He climbed out of his stroller.

Nick concentrated on the data that appeared on the computer screen. He read it out loud. Wayne nodded wisely. He adjusted some dials.

"Adam get Bunny." Adam toddled toward his best friend.

Then Nick saw something on his computer screen that he didn't like at all.

"Dad!" he shrieked.

Wayne looked up. He saw it, too. It was bad. "A power surge!" he called. "Quick! The abort switches!"

Nick searched the panel in front of him. He didn't see anything. It was all a blur!

Loving parents Wayne and Diane Szalinski give their two-year-old son, Adam, his breakfast.

Fourteen-year-old Nick Szalinski helps his father test out his latest invention—a matter-enlarging machine!

No one sees Adam walk right into the path of the enlarging beam.

Nick tries to remain cool as he discovers that Adam's baby-sitter is none other than Mandy Park, the girl of his dreams.

Nick and Mandy try to catch up with Adam before he gets into BIG trouble.

Climbing over a neighbor's wall is child's play for an enlarged Adam.

From atop Adam's colossal Big Bunny, Wayne tries to lull his 112-foot son to sleep.

Nick and Mandy view Las Vegas from the pocket of Adam's jumper.

Mandy hangs on for dear life while Nick moves to rescue her.

People scramble to keep away from Adam's enormous feet.

Mandy and Nick finally take a breather after their night of adventure.

"Where?" he yelled.

"Four of them! Under the red covers!"

There was a loud crack. Suddenly smoke started pouring from one of the computer bays. It had short-circuited!

"Adam want Bunny!" Adam said. He wasn't paying any more attention to Nick and Wayne than they were to him. He just wanted his bunny. He walked over to the pedestal.

Nick hit the red switches. Nothing!

"Five, four, three,..." an electronic voice announced.

Wayne looked at the computer screen. It read Unable to Abort, which meant there was no stopping the experiment. Wayne and Nick both pounded on the keyboard desperately. They never saw what happened next.

"... two, one...," went the electronic voice.

"Uh-oh," Adam said. He was standing right in front of Big Bunny!

Zzzzzzzaaaaaaaaapppppp!

The bright red laser flashed through Wayne's invention and surrounded Adam in a smoky pink aura.

The lights in the lab flickered. Adam sat down. Then the beam zapped Big Bunny. The lights flickered again. Adam crawled back to his stroller.

"Bye-bye, bye-bye," he said. It was the same thing he said whenever he knew he was in big trouble.

Wayne turned around just in time to see the last of the beam hit Big Bunny. Then the beam seemed to withdraw back into Wayne's invention. The machine shut down. When everything was quiet, Wayne walked over to the pedestal and picked up Big Bunny. It didn't seem any different. That meant that test number 1,278 was a failure, too.

Wayne handed Big Bunny to Adam and turned off the remaining lights. They headed for the hall.

When they came around a corner, they found Smitty waiting for them. He seemed embarrassed about what he had to say.

"Mr. Szalinski," he began. "Uh, your security clearance denies you access to the equipment without Dr. Hendrickson's permission. You are aware of that, right?"

Nick was surprised. Wayne wasn't.

"Yes, I know."

"I had to, uh, call Dr. Hendrickson. I'm sorry, Mr. Szalinski."

"It's okay, Smitty. I understand," Wayne said. Smitty had just been doing his job.

Then Smitty looked at Adam and Nick. He hadn't seen Adam for a long time. The baby smiled and waved at Smitty. Smitty waved back. "That baby of yours, he sure is starting to get big!" Smitty said. "Two year olds grow very fast, and sooner than you can believe it, you don't have a baby anymore. You've got

28

a big kid. Why, you should see my grandchildren..."
Smitty said. He liked to talk about his grandchildren.
Wayne didn't have time to hear that now. He knew he
had to get out. Wayne said good-bye to Smitty, and the
three Szalinskis went out to the parking lot. It was time
to go home.

CHAPTER

When the Szalinskis got into the van, it seemed that each one of them had something on his mind.

Wayne shook his head in confusion. "It should have worked," he said. He was sure the lens would have made all the difference.

"Uh, Dad, how come you've got to ask somebody's permission to work on your own invention?" Nick asked.

In the car seat in the back of the van, Adam looked at Big Bunny. "Big . . . big . . . big!" he said.

Wayne tried to answer Nick's question. "Well, uh, see, I'm a member of a team now, Nick."

"But Dad—it's *your* invention. They didn't have the idea, you did."

Wayne couldn't argue with that. Nick was right. But life wasn't always fair, and Wayne wanted to spend some time with Nick to help him try to understand the way things worked.

From the backseat, the baby said, "Adam *big.*"

As he pulled the van into the driveway, Wayne made up his mind to get a baby-sitter for Adam and do something special with Nick that afternoon. They'd have fun. He pulled the van to a stop and turned off the motor.

Nick headed for his room while Wayne reached into the backseat to get Adam.

"Ouch!" he hollered. He'd just about put his back out trying to lift Adam out of the van. "You've put on some weight!" he said to the baby.

"Big," Adam agreed. Then he giggled.

Wayne lugged the baby into the house. "Daddy's going to fix you an early lunch. Maybe something low in calories. And then Nick and Daddy are going out. I'm going to get a baby-sitter so I can spend some quality time with Nick."

Wayne put Adam in his high chair. It creaked. Then Wayne shuffled through the papers on the refrigerator until he found the phone number he wanted. He dialed.

"Hello? Is this . . . uh, Mandy?"

In a few seconds, it was all done. Mandy would be there at 3:30.

Wayne put some food in the microwave for Adam and went to Nick's room to tell him the good news.

As soon as he was alone, Adam slid out of his high chair and toddled over to the microwave. He liked its flashing numbers, and especially its turntable. He put his face very close to the microwave to watch the food spin around inside. And then something odd happened: an electromagnetic force field seemed to shoot out from the microwave and surround Adam in a blanket of bright light.

Adam held Big Bunny up to the oven and the same light surrounded the stuffed animal.

Quark barked. He barked at the funny sound the microwave was making. He barked at Adam's giggles. Mostly, though, he barked at the shadow that Adam was casting on the wall of the kitchen. It was growing!

CHAPTER

When Wayne and Nick came downstairs, they couldn't believe what they saw. It looked like Adam; it talked like Adam; it walked like Adam; it even clutched Big Bunny like Adam. The only difference was that it was seven feet tall!

"Wh-wha—I mean, how?" Nick stuttered.

"This morning... in the lab," Wayne said. "Adam—"

"He was off to the side. I know it!"

Wayne shook his head. "I don't think so," he said. Nick had to agree.

"Adam big," Adam said. He held up Big Bunny. "Big Bunny big, too."

Wayne and Nick thought that was an understatement. They were more than a little nervous to see a two year old who was bigger than they were.

"Don't worry, Adam," Wayne said. "Daddy's going to make everything all right."

Adam didn't seem worried at all. It was Wayne who

was worried. What would he tell Diane? Where would they get clothes for Adam? What would the neighbors say?

"We've got to get him back to the lab. We can analyze the data and reverse the process," Wayne said.

It sounded logical, but there was a problem with it. Nick spotted the problem right away.

"Dad, do you think the guard might get suspicious when we walk in with a seven-foot baby?"

Wayne hadn't thought of that, but he had an idea for a way around it.

An hour later, Wayne and Nick had Adam dressed up in an outfit they bought at the shop for big and tall men at the mall. He was wearing a checkered sports coat and a jungle helmet with mosquito netting. Nobody would ever recognize him as a baby. Of course, they might think he was a giant clown, but Wayne and Nick had to take that chance.

"Just act natural," Wayne instructed Nick as they walked down the hall at Sterling Labs. Under the circumstances, acting natural was going to be the hardest thing Nick had ever done. He whistled casually, but that didn't help.

Then Wayne shushed him up because they weren't alone. They could see Dr. Hendrickson in the lab with two technicians. He didn't look happy.

Wayne told the boys to wait outside.

"Szalinski!" Dr. Hendrickson yelled when he saw him.

Wayne knew something was wrong. "I just stopped by to, uh, check, uh, some computations in the data base."

Dr. Hendrickson's face turned red. He was angry. "The data base has been erased! All thirty-eight gigabytes! Gone!"

This was definitely bad news. That would make it impossible to find out what had happened to Adam that morning. And if they couldn't find out what had happened, it would be very hard to make it unhappen. "That can't be!" Wayne said. He felt faint.

"Sure it can," Dr. Hendrickson said. "*If* the main controller was trying to compensate laser intensity..."

Wayne had an awful feeling he knew what was coming. He was right.

Dr. Hendrickson reached for something on his desk and held it right up in front of Wayne's face. It was the broken bottom of a soda bottle.

"... for *this*, which you jammed into the filter pack, you idiot, causing a power surge through the entire main-drive system!"

Wayne was upset. The machine was messed up, and it was his fault.

At that moment, Adam pushed through the door into the lab. He said something that was hard to understand because Nick had his hand over Adam's mouth.

"Who is this?" Dr. Hendrickson asked.

Wayne said the first thing that came into his head. "A friend."

"What language is he speaking?" Dr. Hendrickson demanded.

"Uh, he's Yugoslavian. He's my uncle Yanosh, see."

"Bah-foom," Adam said.

"Did he say 'bathroom'?" Dr. Hendrickson asked.

"Oh, no, no," Wayne said. "It's *bah-foom*. That's 'pleased to meet you' in Yugoslavia."

"*Bah-foom!*" Dr. Hendrickson said back to Adam.

Wayne didn't want to talk about strange relatives. He wanted to talk about the invention and when he could use it again.

"How long before the system is restored from the backups?" he asked.

"It's of no concern to you," Dr. Hendrickson said. "You're off the project."

Wayne had been expecting Dr. Hendrickson to try to pull something like this. He didn't think Dr. Hendrickson could get away with it, though.

"You don't have the authority to make that decision," Wayne said.

"Maybe I *didn't*," Dr. Hendrickson said. "But after your little charade here this morning"—he waved the soda-bottle bottom at Wayne—"I think old man Sterling will want to give me that authority."

There was nothing for Wayne to do but leave. The boys followed him out of the building and to their van.

CHAPTER  10

"Why didn't you tell him, Dad?" Nick asked as they drove home. Although he was worried about his brother, he was also proud that his father had solved the problem, and he didn't understand why Wayne hadn't told Dr. Hendrickson.

Wayne looked serious. "Remember when we made you kids promise never, ever to tell anyone that you were accidentally shrunk and lost in the backyard for two days?"

Nick would *never* forget that!

His father went on. "That's because we didn't want you to become specimens, to undergo countless tests, to be subjected to endless observation, and to who knows what else."

That made sense to Nick. "But what about Adam?" he asked. "What are we going to do?"

"I don't know," Wayne said. He pulled the van into

the driveway of their house and stopped the motor. "What I do know is that we have to figure out some way to fix this before your mother gets home!"

As if that had been a cue, Diane walked out of the house. She waved cheerfully. "Hi, guys! I'm home!" she said.

CHAPTER

Wayne and Nick froze in their seats. They didn't know what to do. Then Diane smiled and held up Big Bunny. He was *very* big.

"Where did this come from?" she asked.

Wayne didn't think she'd be smiling for long when he told her! Suddenly he couldn't tell her. In fact, the only thing he could do was run. He slammed the van into reverse and pulled back out of the driveway as fast as he could. The van fishtailed backward. When Wayne shifted gears, he left a patch of rubber on the street as he peeled away from the house.

"Mama! Mama!" Adam cried out from the backseat.

"What should we do?" Wayne asked Nick.

Nick had an interesting suggestion. "We could drive to Mexico, Dad, and hide out. Maybe we could come back when Adam's bigger, uh, I mean *older*. Maybe she wouldn't notice then?"

Wayne considered the suggestion. Then he reconsidered it. He just knew it wouldn't work.

"No," he said, finally. "Honesty is the best policy. I'll just, uh, explain." He gulped.

Nick decided to encourage his father. "Sure," he said. "And, when you think about it, it's not the first time something like this has happened. I mean, to *our* family."

"Right! So I'll just tell the truth, plain and simple," Wayne said, sounding braver than he felt. He turned the van around. "And then I'll, uh . . . ," he searched for the right phrase.

Nick supplied it. "Beg for mercy," he said.

Wayne pulled the van back into the driveway and got out. Diane was waiting for him. She was very confused.

"What was *that* all about?" she asked.

"Hmmm?" Wayne stalled. "Oh, uh, just a little trouble with the van. Thought I put it in park, but it was in reverse." Wayne took a deep breath. He stalled, "Well, honey, uh, gee. Back early, huh?"

Diane looked at the van. She was suspicious, but she didn't see anything unusual. The bright sunshine glared across the windshield, making it difficult for her to see inside. Still, she'd lived with Wayne Szalinski long enough to know when he was trying to cover something up.

"I, uh, took a cab from the airport," Diane explained. "It turned out that Amy really didn't need me.

I felt kind of silly." She shifted to the right to get a better view of what was going on in the van. She saw something. "Who's the tall man in the loud sports coat?" she asked.

Wayne pasted a confident smile on his face and put his arm around his wife's shoulders. He led her toward the house—away from the van.

"Well now, honey," he began, "that's something I have to explain." But *how* he wondered. "Hey. You're probably going to get a big laugh out of this. . . . " *Sure,* he thought to himself, *right after you strangle me. . . .* He opened the door to the house and led Diane inside. At least there she couldn't *see* the van rocking and *hear* the muffled shouts of her oversize two year old.

"Mama! Go see Mama!"

"No!" Nick said, trying to shush his brother.

Inside the house, Wayne was having trouble getting to the point.

"You know how, sometimes, things I invent don't always work the way they're supposed to?" Wayne said.

Diane knew something was definitely wrong. Being married to Wayne Szalinski meant that things often went wrong. Nowadays, however, it also meant making him try to feel better about it. "Sweetheart, whatever it is, you can tell me," she assured him. "How bad could it be? After all, it's not like you did something to one of the kids again, is it?"

Wayne gulped. Diane smelled a rat.

41

"Hey, where *are* the kids?" she asked.

"Uh . . . ," Wayne began.

Diane eyed the door. "And who was that in the van?" she asked.

"Uh . . . uh . . . "

A thought crossed Diane's mind. She didn't like it at all. "And where did that giant Big Bunny come from?" she asked.

That was all Wayne could take. "*All right! I confess! I did it!*" he shrieked.

"Did what?" Diane asked.

At that moment, the front door flew open. There stood Adam—all seven feet of him.

"Mama!" he said.

That was when Wayne admitted it: "Honey, I blew up the kid. . . ."

Diane did the only logical thing under the circumstances. She fainted.

Nick peered around the door. "How did she take it?" he asked.

"Oh, about like usual," Wayne told him.

Wayne picked Diane up and carried her to the sofa in the living room. He fanned her to give her fresh air and told Nick to look after Adam until Diane recovered. Nick took Adam into the dining room, where Adam took the opportunity to jump on all his toys and smash them to smithereens.

"Nick! What's he doing?" Wayne called into the dining room.

"Jumping on his toys, Dad," Nick explained.

"Well, make him stop," Wayne said.

"Make him stop," Nick muttered to himself while Adam lined up an entire family of action figures and squished them flat. "Why didn't *I* think of that?" He spoke in his sternest older brother voice, "All right, Adam, this is your last warning. Stop jumping on your toys."

Adam bounced on a fire-truck set. Firemen flew all over the room, pelting Nick.

"All right," Nick said, "I'll give you one more warning. . . ."

Diane came to. She remembered what had happened. She screamed.

"Honey, shhhhh," Wayne said. "It isn't as bad as it seems." He hugged her to comfort her.

Nick ran into the living room. "I finally got him in his room," he said.

"Tell him he has to stay in there and close his door," said Wayne.

"I did close his door," Nick said.

Then there was a crash, followed by a series of loud thumps. Adam walked into the living room. He was carrying the door to his room.

"I think he just opened the door," Nick said.

CHAPTER 12

It wasn't easy keeping a two year old occupied, especially when the two year old was seven feet tall. The Szalinskis tried dancing the hokey pokey. Adam liked that, but the whole house shook every time he put his whole self in!

While Diane and Nick played with Adam, Wayne went to work. He turned the entire living room into a giant version of Adam's playpen. Diane and Nick lured Adam into it, but when Adam looked around at the screens, noisemakers, and toys, he made a face. He knew a playpen when he saw one.

Diane couldn't believe what Wayne had done this time. How did he keep getting the family into such messes?

Nick stood up for his dad. "You have to admit, Mom, there aren't too many guys who could whip up an invention like the giant playpen in thirty minutes."

Diane knew that was true, but then there weren't a

lot of guys who would *have* to do it, either. Diane looked over at Wayne. He was sitting at the dining room table, filling pages of yellow paper with numbers and formulas. The calculations seemed to go on for miles, but none of them seemed to make him happy. Wayne looked very worried.

Diane had to know. "Wayne?" she asked.

He smiled weakly. "Uh, well, the answer might be in the atomic . . . uh. Well, some of the numbers indicate . . ."

Diane knew a bluff when she heard one. "The truth, sweetheart. Okay?"

"The truth is, Diane, without access to the data at the plant, there's not much I can do. I know what's happening, but I don't know why." He was very sad. "I'm sorry, honey," he said. He shook his head.

"Hey, look!" Nick said. "I found a way to keep him quiet!" He held up an empty box of ice-cream bars.

Diane was astonished. "There were twelve ice-cream bars in there!"

"*Burp*," said Adam.

"Well, he's just about ruined his dinner," Diane remarked sourly.

Nick crinkled his eyebrows, just the way his father did when he was thinking hard. "Not necessarily, Mom," Nick said. "At his body weight, he should be able to metabolize . . . " He could see by the look on his mother's face that she didn't want to hear the news. He closed his mouth.

Diane looked at Wayne. She felt sorry for him, but she felt sorrier for Adam. They had to do something, *any*thing.

"Let's take him to the lab, Wayne," she said. "Hopefully there are people there who . . ."

She stopped because she didn't like what she was about to say. Wayne finished the sentence for her.

"Who know what they're doing?"

"I didn't mean it that way," Diane said. "I'm sorry, Wayne, but all I want right now is to see my baby shrink down to his normal size."

"Shrink, shrink," Wayne said. He repeated the word over and over as if it had never occurred to him. "I've got an idea!" he shouted. "My original machine! They have it stored in the lab's security warehouse."

Nick saw what his father was getting at. "Yes!" he howled.

Wayne leaned toward Diane and spoke urgently. "This will have to be a covert operation. Diane, you have to go with me. Nick, you stay here with Adam."

"What? Leave them alone?" Diane said.

"Diane, listen," Wayne said. "You can't take him to the lab. There's no telling what Dr. Hendrickson will do if he gets his hands on Adam. To him, the baby will be just another research specimen!"

"He's right, Mom," Nick agreed. "That guy is a major creep."

Diane didn't like the idea of leaving Adam. On the other hand, Wayne needed her. On the third hand,

Adam was yawning. He was ready for an "N-A-P," and all it took was a good cuddle with Big Bunny, the gentle, loving hug of his mother, a few verses of "Alouette" from his father, and Adam was sleeping soundly.

Diane and Wayne headed for the warehouse. They both knew that it was their only chance to save Adam from the prying eyes of scientists.

CHAPTER

At Sterling Laboratories, two technicians worked furiously at the computer console. They wanted to know exactly what had happened in the lab that morning, and it was going to take a lot of work to find out. The data was there, somewhere. It was just hard to see.

The image on the screen was vague, but they could tell that the machine had been used that morning. Then they saw that the beams of light coming from it had touched *some*thing. But what was it? At first, all they could see was a two-and-a-half-foot-tall target that got zapped with the beam. But when they pushed some more buttons, the picture became clearer—and odder.

"Look, there it is," one technician said. "And it's got three eyes. . . ."

"And fuzzy white arms?"

"A new life-form?"

"This could be big. . . ."

* * *

Wayne drove as fast as he could through town, but when he reached the warehouse parking lot, he was much more careful. He parked his van between two big trucks so nobody could see it. Then he and Diane got out and walked to the warehouse on tiptoe.

The side door was open. They sneaked in.

"They stored all my stuff, everything, in one large crate," Wayne said to Diane. "It should be easy to spot."

Except that the warehouse was a half mile long! They had their work cut out for them.

Meanwhile, back at the Szalinski house . . .

Ding-dong!

Adam's eyes flickered. Nick couldn't let him wake up!

"*Alouette, gentille alouette . . .*" Nick whispered. Adam sighed and went back to sleep.

Ding-dong!

Nick ran for the door. He couldn't let it ring again! He pulled it open and there was—

"Mandy!"

"Rick?"

"Nick. Nick Szalinski."

"Right."

Nick couldn't believe his eyes. What was Mandy doing at his house—today of all days?

"I'm here to baby-sit," she said.

Nick remembered that he and his father had planned to go to a movie. But that was before everything happened.

"We don't need a baby-sitter," Nick said. He closed the door.

Ding-dong!

A loud thumping came from the living room. "Uh-oh, doorbell!" Adam cried.

That was when Mandy decided to lean on the doorbell. It rang insistently. Nick had to do something. He opened the door, stepped out, and slammed it behind him.

"Very funny," Mandy said. "Now can I come in? I'm already charging you."

"We changed our mind," Nick said. "We don't need a baby-sitter." He didn't add that right then a gorilla-sitter would have been more appropriate.

Mandy did not change her mind. "I need eight more dollars to see the rock concert next week, and I was promised three hours at two-fifty an hour, plus extra if I'm grossed out."

The door behind Nick buckled under pressure from Adam. Nick held the handle and tried to hold his ground.

"Listen, Mandy. Take it from me. You don't want to baby-sit. Not *this* baby."

"Like, I'm really sure I can't handle some stupid baby..."

Then the door opened. Adam smiled broadly. He

was rested and cheerful. "Hi! What you name?" he asked.

Mandy fainted.

"Uh-oh."

Meanwhile, back in the warehouse . . .

Wayne and Diane were surrounded by endless stacks of crates.

"Wayne, we have to get back! There's just no way we're going to find it."

Wayne was about to agree with Diane when he spotted the very thing he was looking for. It was a big crate with his name stenciled on the side.

"Honey, it's up here!"

And, in the nearby laboratory . . .

The two technicians still huddled over the screen. Vague images began to form as the program worked to clarify what the camera had recorded.

"Look at this—a second set of arms! They're human!"

The first technician picked up the phone. "Well, Dr. Hendrickson, we, uh, think we know. But it might be better if you saw it for yourself. . . ."

CHAPTER 14

Adam liked television. He was happy sitting and watching cartoons. Big Bunny was watching with him.

Nick paced around the kitchen, trying to talk sense into Mandy.

"Believe me, Mandy, everything is under control...."

At least *Mandy* was under control. She was totally controlled. She was tied to a kitchen chair and had a gag in her mouth!

"...Now, I'll take the gag out of your mouth if you promise you won't scream. Promise?"

Mandy nodded. Nick took the gag off. Mandy screamed. Then she screamed some more. Finally, Mandy stopped screaming. "Man, I've been at this for ten minutes. You can kiss off neighborhood watch around *here*."

The neighbors were accustomed to having weird

things happen in the Szalinski house, so nobody came to investigate. Adam was too interested in his television show to notice.

"Mandy, despite what he looks like, Adam is just a little kid. He's in there watching TV, not hurting anybody."

In the living room, the cartoon finished and a man on the screen began exercising. It looked like a fun dance to Adam, so he started to dance, too. He wanted to see the screen better, and he brought Big Bunny closer to the television. Then, just to be sure they could see everything, Adam put his face—and Big Bunny's—right up next to the picture.

There was a buzzing and an electronic whine. A glow emanated from the television and enveloped Adam and Big Bunny. It tickled. Adam laughed.

Nick finished telling Mandy about his father and his fantastic invention.

"Now, let me see if I've got this straight," Mandy said. "Two years ago, he made you and your sister tiny?"

"And the guys next door," Nick said.

"Then he made you regular-size again. And now he's made your baby brother big?"

"That's right."

"And you don't, like, think that's unusual?"

That wasn't an easy question for Nick to answer. Fortunately, he didn't have to answer it right then. He was interrupted by a loud sound. The whole house seemed to shake.

Ka-boom! Ka-boom!

"All right! Get those legs pumping!" the man on the television said. Adam was trying to do it. It wasn't easy, though, because he was fourteen feet tall and the ceiling was only nine feet high!

CHAPTER

"I think I've got it now!"

Diane hoped Wayne knew what he was talking about. She was at the wheel of their van. Wayne was in the back, trying to fit the parts of his invention together. He was working furiously, and she was driving furiously. She was feeling furious, too.

"This is it! This is *really* it! No more Mr. Wizard! No more subscription to *Popular Science*! I'm not kidding!"

Diane was so furious that she wasn't paying very much attention to her driving. For instance, she wasn't paying very much attention to the speedometer.

There were two motorcycle policemen nearby. They *were* paying attention, and they could hardly believe what their radar gun told them. Diane was driving seventy-five miles per hour! They kick started their engines and turned on their sirens.

*   *   *

Things weren't going much better back at the Szalinski house. Adam had gotten bored with the exercise show and wanted to play outdoors, so he broke out of the house, shattering the door as he left. He wandered over to the Szalinskis' neighbor's yard, where a birthday party was in progress. The mother of the birthday boy was trying to be a magician. She wasn't very good. The children made faces. She tried harder.

"All right, boys and girls, look at the bunny!" she said.

Adam had a bunny. It was a big bunny. And when he held him up so all the children could see it, the children looked surprised. The mother thought it was because of the little stuffed bunny she had. Then Adam stood up and the children could see how tall he was. They began shrieking. The mother didn't know what was so scary about her little stuffed bunny. She turned around.

"Hi!" Adam said.

The mother screamed and ran, too.

When Nick and Mandy heard the screams, they knew where they could find Adam.

A big black limousine was coming down the street where the Szalinskis lived. Dr. Hendrickson was in the backseat. He was talking on the car phone.

"I don't care where Clifford Sterling is! Find him and get him here. I also want the entire board of directors!"

The car screeched to a halt. That annoyed Dr. Hen-

56

drickson. He was in a hurry to get to Wayne's house. He rolled down the window and saw that there were a lot of screaming children. Then he saw that there was a screaming mother, too. He began yelling at them. He often yelled before he knew what he was yelling about.

"What the devil's wrong with you?" he demanded.

Then he saw. He grabbed for the phone again.

"Contact the federal marshals! Get them out here! I want this neighborhood sealed off! And heavy equipment—something large enough to hold . . . " For a second, he couldn't think how to describe it. Then he continued, ". . . to hold something very big."

Sirens roared. The policemen were catching up with Diane, but as long as the sun remained bright, she thought she could outrun them. Then there was a cloud.

"Uh, Wayne? I'm having trouble with this situation. This isn't happening! What do I do?"

From the rear of the van, Wayne tightened one more bolt and welded a few last things in place.

"I wonder if this thing still works," he mused. He flipped a few switches.

Zzzzzzzaaaaaaaaapppppp!

A laser shot out of the rear of the van, seeking a target. It found just what it wanted in two motorcycle policemen. Diane saw it all in the rearview mirror. Where there had been two perfectly normal cops, now there were two matchbox-size officers of the law. Trying to run away from them was one thing, but this was something else.

"Wayne Szalinski! You unshrink those policemen before you get us into trouble!"

Zzzzzzzaaaaaaaaappppp!

The policemen popped back up to full size. They drew their motorcycles to a screeching halt.

"They're getting away," one of them said.

"I can accept that," the other one said.

CHAPTER 16

By the time Wayne and Diane got back to their neighborhood, everything was going wild. Streets were closed and roped off. Hundreds of emergency vehicles had flashing lights going like crazy.

Wayne and Diane jumped out of their van and ran to the two people who seemed to be in charge. One was Dr. Hendrickson. The other was a federal marshal.

"Where are my boys?! Where are they?!" Diane demanded.

The marshal held Quark by the scuff of his neck. "Preston Brooks," he said, introducing himself. "We found the mutt hiding in a garage down the street. Your children are quite safe, Mrs. Szalinski. We needed to get the baby some room so he wouldn't hurt himself."

Then Dr. Hendrickson said the very words the Szalinskis had been dreading, "Of course, the mutated child will have to undergo immediate testing. We're taking him to a special lab in the desert. We made a gigantic playpen for him. He's safe. He can't get out of it."

"A playpen?" Wayne and Diane said together. This was *big* trouble.

Then Dr. Hendrickson said some more things the Szalinskis didn't want to hear. "I'm afraid I have to insist that these two be taken into custody."

But before anybody could arrest them, another car arrived on the scene. It was a very big, very shiny limousine. It was Dr. Sterling himself.

Dr. Hendrickson seemed very happy to see Dr. Sterling. He always liked a chance to make other people look bad in front of the boss. This situation was tailor-made for that!

Dr. Hendrickson oozed his way over to Dr. Sterling's car.

"Clifford," he said. "I hardly know what to say. I tried to warn you about Szalinski from the very beginning."

Dr. Sterling smiled at him. "Yes, you did," he said. "I didn't see what you were getting at then, but I do now."

Wayne couldn't wait any longer. "Dr. Sterling!" he called out. "I can reverse my son's growth."

"You can?"

"Just give me a chance. I know I can do it. I can get him back to normal."

"With what, Wayne?" Dr. Hendrickson asked. He was sneering. "Soda bottles? Maybe a little chewing gum and twine?" Then he turned to Dr. Sterling. "Clifford, the situation demands that I bring in people who have the expertise *and* the credentials . . ."

That made Wayne very angry. He put his hands on his hips and said some things to Dr. Hendrickson that he'd been waiting to say for months. "All right! So I'm just some guy who tinkered with crackpot ideas in his attic!" Then he turned to Dr. Sterling. "But, let me tell you something. This country is standing on the shoulders of people who tinkered with crackpot ideas in attics and basements and backyards! Alexander Graham Bell, working in his two-room flat, he's just one of—"

"Young man!" Clifford Sterling cut Wayne off. "Don't presume to stand there and lecture me. I've never been a fool, and I don't intend to start being one now."

Wayne looked down at the ground. Things were not looking good for him, but they were looking even worse for his children.

Dr. Sterling turned to Dr. Hendrickson then. "Charles," he said.

"Yes, Clifford?" Dr. Hendrickson answered eagerly.

"You're fired."

Suddenly, things were looking much better for all the Szalinskis!

"Now, Wayne," Dr. Sterling said. "Why don't you tell

61

me what you have in mind so we can get that kid of yours back to normal size by bedtime."

Wayne was about to do just that when all the police radios began crackling an emergency code at the same time. The news was no surprise to Wayne and Diane. Adam had broken out of the playpen. He'd left Big Bunny behind and was walking through the desert.

CHAPTER 17

"He did *what*?!" Diane asked. She and Wayne were driving through the desert as fast as they could in their van. Marshal Brooks and Dr. Sterling were with them. Marshal Brooks had his radio with him. Diane wasn't sure she was happy to be getting such up-to-the-minute reports.

Marshal Brooks repeated the news. "He escaped. Then he got bigger. Your son Nick and the girl he's with, they tried to get him to sit down, but he just leaned over and picked them up and put them in his pocket."

That sounded just like Adam. He was forever putting odd things in his pockets. But his *brother*?

"What's causing this growth phenomenon?" Dr. Sterling asked Wayne.

Wayne scratched his head. "I don't know. I . . . hmmm. Maybe. Ah, yes. Maybe. They were transporting him along Copper Mine Road. It runs alongside high-voltage lines. Then, earlier, when he first grew, we were using the microwave . . . of course!"

"I don't get it," Diane said.

"Electromagnetic flux!" Dr. Sterling explained. That didn't explain anything to Diane, however.

"There's a sort of electrical field around any electrical device," Wayne explained. "It's a force field."

Then Marshal Brooks had a question. "Uh, would this flux thing surround neon lights, too?"

"Sure it would," Wayne said.

"Then I think we'd better hurry because the kid is headed straight for Las Vegas!"

Marshal Brooks got on his radio and issued a lot of orders very fast. He had his men set up a roadblock on the only road that Adam could follow into Las Vegas, a city with millions of neon lights.

Wayne was busy, too. He climbed into the back of the van and began pushing buttons and working on his formulas.

"By my calculations, all he has to do is hold still for five point two seconds . . ."

"What?" Diane asked. There was something she didn't like about what Wayne had said. "Just how do you expect to get a two year old to hold still for five point *anything* seconds?"

Wayne stopped pushing buttons. "She's right," he said to Dr. Sterling. "We tried to have his picture taken a month ago. It was a total bust."

But they had to figure out a way to do it. They just *had* to!

Then there was a new sound in the desert. *Ka-boom! Ka-boom!*

All four of the people in the van looked out. They couldn't believe what they were seeing. It was Adam, all right. And he was fifty-six feet tall!

"Wayne, he looks like he's okay," Diane said. "But is this going to affect him for life? Something like this could ruin a kid!"

Wayne had a way of looking on the bright side of things. "Now, honey, it'll probably just help him to see the big picture."

Two people who already had a close-up view of the big picture were Nick and Mandy. They were still in the front pocket of Adam's overalls, getting quite a ride!

It was dark in the desert, and searchlights followed Adam with every giant step he took. Nick and Mandy held on tight. Mandy wished she were someplace else. Anyplace. She even wished she'd taken the job baby-sitting the Feldman twins today, and they were *awful*! Anything was better than this.

"You know, Nick, I'm really glad I met you," she said sarcastically.

"You are?" Even though Nick was actually more than four stories above the desert, in the middle of a totally hopeless situation, he didn't seem to be able to forget that he was also right next to Mandy. He'd been dreaming about being next to her for a long time, and now she seemed happy about it, too.

"Sure," she said. "Who else would have taken me out for a ride in his little brother's pocket?" Well, maybe she wasn't all *that* happy about it.

When Nick shaded his eyes against the bright lights, he could just barely make out his father's weird van down below. That made him feel much better. As long as his father was around, things were going to get better. At least he was pretty sure they would, anyway.

Suddenly there was a jolt. Nick and Mandy held on for their lives while Adam leaned over to pick something up. It was an emergency road sign. He picked it up. He looked at it. He liked the bright orange that shone in the light. But when he moved it out of the light, it stopped shining. That wasn't any fun. He threw it back down to the ground.

Down below, Marshal Brooks suggested that they try to use rope guns to tie Adam up.

"Absolutely not!" Diane said. "You're not shooting anything at my baby!"

"Right!" Wayne added. "We're his parents and we know how to take care of him. Don't we, Diane?" Wayne wasn't really so sure about the last part. What could they do? Then he thought of something that could help.

"Big Bunny," he said to Marshal Brooks. "We need Big Bunny."

Marshal Brooks got on the radio. Within a very short time, Big Bunny was delivered to the desert, and suspended from a helicopter. It wasn't just Big Bunny anymore. It was Very Big Bunny. Adam jumped joyfully and clapped his hands when he saw his favorite toy.

Inside Adam's pocket, Mandy wasn't so happy.

"I swear I'm going to barf if he doesn't stop," she said.

"Stop it, Adam!" Nick commanded. It didn't do any good. "I'm positive my dad has a plan to get us—"

"I don't believe I'm seeing this," Mandy said.

Nick couldn't believe it, either. There was Big Bunny, being held by a helicopter, and there, sitting on Big Bunny's head, was none other than Wayne Szalinski. Wayne was wearing a crash helmet, and he had a megaphone in his hand.

"I told you my dad would have a plan," Nick said smugly.

Then the sound began to come over the megaphone.

"*Alouette, gentille alouette. Alouette, je te plumerai . . .*"

The look on Mandy's face said it all. Nick was sure he was adopted.

Down on the ground, Diane spoke to Dr. Sterling. "Get ready. His eyes are blinking. He always does that right before he goes to sleep."

Dr. Sterling pointed the machine at Adam. He was ready.

The helicopter lowered Very Big Bunny toward the ground. Wayne held on tight.

Adam sat down and reached for Very Big Bunny. His eyes blinked.

"That's right, Adam. Time for a nice long..."

"No! Don't say it, Wayne!" Diane screamed, but it was too late.

"...nap."

Adam sat up abruptly. "No nap! No! No!"

He swatted angrily at Very Big Bunny. The stuffed animal and Wayne swung back and forth wildly.

"Dad!" Nick shrieked. He had a very good view of his father and knew that things were looking bad.

"Don't worry, Nick. Everything's under control," Wayne promised him as he swung in a sixty-foot arc. It wasn't true at all. Adam hit Very Big Bunny one more time, and that was all Wayne could take. He slid off the stuffed animal and fell—right onto Adam's shirt and down his front—inside his overalls!

As he fell toward Adam's waist, his last words to Nick and Mandy were, "There's absolutely nothing to worry about, kids."

"Gee, I feel a *whole* lot better," Mandy said.

Ka-boom! Ka-boom!

"Adam Szalinski! You stop this *right* now!" Diane yelled as loudly as she could. It didn't do any good. Then she tried it with the bullhorn. *"ADAM! THIS IS MOMMY TALKING! STOP!!!"*

Nothing happened. "I'm afraid that won't do any good, Mrs. Szalinski," Dr. Sterling said. "He expects his mommy to be bigger than he is. He wants to go to Las Vegas, and nothing is going to stop him—certainly not a pint-size mom."

It hurt Diane very much to know that her baby didn't even recognize her. She wanted to cry, but there was too much work to do.

Dr. Hendrickson had called in the Nevada State Militia. He would stop at nothing to capture Adam Szalinski. He just had to prove to everybody that he knew what he was doing. He was right, and nothing would stop him.

Captain Ed Meyerson helped him load a big piece of equipment onto a helicopter. "What is this thing?" he asked.

"It's a tranquilizer cannon," Dr. Hendrickson explained.

Meyerson made a face. He didn't like the idea at all.

Then the radio crackled to life with an updated news report.

"*. . . observers on the scene report that the baby has once more doubled in size . . .*"

Dr. Hendrickson patted the tranquilizer cannon. It was just what the doctor ordered! "Let's get going!" he said.

There it was! All those lights! Adam couldn't believe his eyes. They were beautiful! There were lights in plenty of different colors, and a lot of them flashed on and off. They looked like they were moving. Some of them were shaped like different things, too! Adam saw a boot made out of lights. He liked that. Then there was a horseshoe and a piece of shining gold. There was a boat with a moving paddle wheel and a volcano! He liked the cowboy best. Adam had been a cowboy for Halloween. He thought his costume was almost as nice as this one. He started walking over to the cowboy very fast.

"Clear the street! Clear the street!" a loudspeaker warned the people who were in Adam's path.

Some of them didn't take the warning very seriously.

"Hey, what's happening?" a man asked his wife. "Is Wayne Newton in town?"

"They don't do that for Wayne Newton," she said. "It must be someone bigger than Wayne Newton."

"Nobody's bigger than Wayne Newton in *this* town," the man said.

Suddenly a very large shadow came across their path. The man reconsidered.

"Of course, I could be wrong."

It was Adam. He was now 112 feet tall. That was as tall as a ten-story building! But with all that electricity around, he wasn't going to be just 112 feet tall for long.

Nick and Mandy watched everything from their hideout in Adam's pocket. Nick didn't like what he saw. They had to do something.

"I've got a plan," he said.

"Is it as good as the plan your father had?" Mandy asked. She wasn't convinced the Szalinskis were entirely sane.

"Better," Nick assured her.

"Great. For a second I was worried."

"See, we'll pull the thread out of the seam at the bottom of the pocket and use it for a rope, and we can slide down . . ."

"Say what?" She was quickly becoming convinced that they were all crazy. And now she was afraid she might catch it, too.

Down in the street, Wayne and Diane were just as worried. They knew that if Adam got too close to the lights, he'd blow up some more. And he seemed really interested in the lights. They had to find something that would be even more interesting to him.

Then Wayne spotted just the thing. It was an ice-cream truck. Adam couldn't resist ice cream. Everybody knew that.

"Uh, who can drive an ice-cream truck really fast?" Wayne asked. Marshal Brooks volunteered.

Dr. Sterling shook his head. He was worried about something. "You know, Wayne, if Adam gets much bigger, I don't think we stand a chance of controlling him."

Diane answered for both of them. "Don't worry, Dr. Sterling, we couldn't control him when he was the right size."

Nobody found that comforting.

Mandy thought Nick's idea was pretty flaky, but she didn't have anything better in mind. Together, the two of them tugged at the threads at the bottom of Adam's pocket until they found a loose one. It unraveled quickly, leaving a big hole in the bottom of Adam's pocket, and the next thing they knew, they had yards of thread that looked like rope. Then their moment came.

Adam stumbled on his shoelace. He fell forward and landed on his hands and knees.

Nick held his breath. Mandy closed her eyes. They both gripped the rope tightly and jumped out of Adam's pocket. In a split second, they were suspended over an abandoned convertible. It was perfect.

"Go for it!" Nick yelled. They both let go and landed safely in the car. Nick was in the driver's seat. Mandy was right next to him.

"Get going, Nick!!!" she instructed.

It was one thing to say, but quite another to do. Nick didn't have the vaguest idea how to drive the car. He started pushing buttons. The windshield wipers worked. So did the spritzer for the windshield. The stereo started blasting and the top of the convertible began closing.

"Play cars!" Adam said. He grabbed the car and began running it around in circles.

"*Brrrrvvvvvvvvrrroooooooom!*" he said as he played with it.

Nick and Mandy reached for the seat belts.

Cars were fun, but airplanes were even better. Adam lifted the car into the air. Up and down, around and around.

Nick and Mandy turned green.

On the ground, Wayne yelled into a walkie-talkie, "Where's that ice-cream truck?!"

"We're set!" Marshal Brooks informed him.

Then Wayne looked up to see what was happening. It wasn't good news.

"No! Wait!" he told Marshal Brooks.

Adam had put the car down—right on top of one of the big electric signs! Nick and Mandy were sixty feet above the street, and the car looked like it was about to fall off its perch!

The car teetered to the left. Nick and Mandy leaned right. The car shifted backward. Nick and Mandy leaned forward.

The car tipped forward. Nick and Mandy froze.

That was all the shifting Mandy could take. She just *had* to get out of there. She unclasped her seat belt and opened the door. The car slipped radically to the right. Mandy began to fall.

Nick grabbed her hand. He held on tight. She held on tighter. She began to pull him out of the car, too! He hooked his foot into the steering wheel to stop his fall. Then he pulled with all his might, but he wasn't sure it would be enough. Slowly, he pulled Mandy back into the car. She shut the door and held on tight. Then the car shifted again, and Nick thought this would be the end. His foot hit the horn.

Adam hadn't heard them screaming, but he did hear the horn. He looked at the car.

"Uh-oh, faw down!" he said.

And that's just what the car did. It totally lost its balance and began tumbling into a free-fall!

"Uh-oh!" Adam said again. This time he did something, though. He caught the car!

Nick and Mandy sighed with relief until Adam put the car in his pocket.

"He's always been possessive," Diane explained.

Wayne flicked the switch on his walkie-talkie. "Let her roll!" he said. On that signal, neon lights up and down the streets of Las Vegas went dark. Searchlights cut through the night, and they all focused on an ice-cream truck. Marshal Brooks turned a dial in the truck, and familiar music blared from its speakers.

Marshal Brooks popped the clutch in the truck. The wheels spun and then caught.

"Ice cream!" Adam boomed with delight. He started chasing after the ice-cream truck. The race was on!

CHAPTER

Marshal Brooks was shaken. He could barely control his voice as he spoke into the walkie-talkie.

"Next thing I know, he grabs the big wooden ice-cream bar off the top of the truck. Well, what do *you* think he did with it?"

There, lying in the desert, was a big wooden ice-cream bar. One large bite had been taken out of it.

"Well, that didn't work," Dr. Sterling said to Wayne and Diane. "What are we going to do now?"

"We need to get to Adam, and we need to get him to hold still!" Then she thought for a minute. "You remember how we finally got Adam to hold still to have his picture taken? I sat there and held him?"

Wayne had an idea of what she was getting at, and he wasn't sure he liked it.

Diane went on, "He needs me. He needs me to tell him what he can do and what he can't do. What's okay and what's not. You know, to be a mommy? The problem is that as far as Adam is concerned, his mommy is somebody very much bigger than he is. . . ."

"No way," Wayne said. "It's a crazy idea."

Diane wondered what was so bad about that. Wayne was always having crazy ideas. Why couldn't she have one?

Diane began to say just that to Wayne when there was a noise overhead. It was a helicopter. Wayne looked up at it. There was something awfully familiar about the man in the rear. Could it be Dr. Hendrickson? Wayne hoped he was wrong and decided not to say anything. He had too much to do to worry about things he couldn't change, and besides, they didn't have a minute to waste.

"Preheating the lasers, Wayne!" Dr. Sterling called.

Wayne turned to Diane. He wanted to talk her out of this.

"I should be doing it, not you," he said.

"There's one thing every little kid knows, Wayne. Daddies mean fun. Mommies mean business."

He couldn't argue with that, but this was dangerous. "This machine was never meant to do anything like this. Too little power and you'll grow too slowly, like Adam. Too much power and—" he remembered Dr. Hendrickson's blue crystal. He couldn't go on.

"I trust you, Wayne Szalinski. Heaven help me, I do." She smiled at him then. It was a special smile. "And besides, you're the smartest guy I know."

Wayne smiled back. "Which says a lot about—"

She gave him a little kiss before he could finish the sentence.

The helicopter circled above them again. This time there was no mistaking it. It *was* Dr. Hendrickson, and he had a giant gun of some kind pointed right at Adam!

"Time to get big, Wayne," Diane said.

In the back of the helicopter, Dr. Hendrickson was getting the tranquilizer cannon ready.

"Hey, you're not actually going to use that thing on the kid, are you?" Meyerson, the helicopter's pilot, asked.

"Whatever it takes," Dr. Hendrickson said.

Meyerson looked at Dr. Hendrickson carefully. He saw something in the man's eyes that he didn't like and didn't trust. But he didn't know what to do about it. For now, he just kept on flying, circling the city of Las Vegas and the giant kid who was walking through it.

Adam spotted something that he really wanted. It was a guitar, and it looked just like the one Nick had. Adam had fun with Nick's guitar, and he was sure he would have fun with this one, too.

Of course, Nick's guitar was just a regular electric guitar. But this one was made of neon and was thirty feet long!

"Adam sing!" the two year old cried.

Nick and Mandy peered out of Adam's pocket. Nick

could tell what was on Adam's mind. There were a lot of things Nick didn't think he was old enough for. Electrocution was one of them. Watching Adam get any bigger was another.

Adam plucked the guitar from the wall of the building. The flexible tubes of light didn't break, and the guitar still glowed as he held it. But then Adam started to glow as well.

"Big ow-wee, Adam!" Mandy screamed.

Adam giggled. He didn't hear her at all.

One of the reasons he couldn't hear her was because of all the racket Meyerson's helicopter was making. Nick and Mandy didn't know that Dr. Hendrickson was inside it. For now, all they knew was that the helicopter couldn't possibly be as dangerous as the guitar was.

Then Adam spotted the helicopter, and it delighted him even more than the guitar.

"Air-pane!" he said, trying to grab it out of the air.

"Yeah, Adam!" Nick called. "Nice airplane! Put the guitar down and go get the nice airplane!"

In the helicopter, Dr. Hendrickson began barking orders. "Bring me into range and hold it steady."

"Wait a minute," Meyerson said. "If we hit him and he stumbles, he could fall into that whole crowd of people down there!"

"Then we'll just have to hope he doesn't," Dr. Hendrickson said.

"Air-pane!" said Adam.

"Now!" said Dr. Hendrickson.

Just as Dr. Hendrickson took final aim and fired, the helicopter lunged down and to the right. The tranquilizer dart hit the guitar in Adam's hands. Scared by the gunfire, Adam dropped the guitar, which went crashing to the ground.

"Hey you! Pick on somebody your own size!" Mandy shrieked at the men in the helicopter.

Adam screamed, "No! Air-pane!" Giant tears formed in his baby eyes, his lips quivered, and he began to wail. The booming cry of Adam's sad voice echoed across the desert.

This was just what Dr. Hendrickson needed. His target was still. Now he could shoot.

"Hold it steady," he said to Meyerson.

And at that instant, everything stopped. The rotors on the helicopter had been silenced by a hand, a very big hand. It was a big hand with a nice manicure and a sparkling wedding ring. It was the hand of Adam's mother.

"Back off!" Diane ordered.

"Yes, ma'am," Meyerson agreed quickly. He shut down the engine. Diane set the helicopter down in the desert, quite far away.

Then Adam spotted his mother. He stopped crying and looked up at her. His cheeks were streaked with tears, but there was a smile on his face. Being big was fun. You got to play with all kinds of neat things, ice-cream trucks, moving cars with horns, electric guitars.

But he'd missed his mother, and now she was here.

"Mama!"

"Is that your mom?" Mandy asked, stunned.

"Yeah," Nick said. He was glad to see her, too.

"*Weird* family," Mandy said.

"Come here, baby," Diane said.

Adam ran to his mother while the ground around him shook, and Mandy and Nick were bounced around in his pocket. They even lost their grip on the top seam and tumbled to the bottom of the pocket. They couldn't see Diane, and she couldn't see them.

Diane knelt down on the ground and reached for Adam. She picked him up and gave him a hug. She kissed his cheek and patted his bottom. She'd missed her baby as much as he'd missed his mother! Then she cried, too.

"Everything's going to be okay, Adam. Mommy's here now."

"Mommy cwying?" Adam said. It frightened him a little to see that, but Diane reassured him.

"Yes, dear. Mommy's crying. It's okay to cry when you're happy, and I'm happy to be with you."

She gave him another hug. That squished Nick and Mandy. "Easy, Mom!" Nick yelled up at her, but she couldn't hear him.

Down below, the scientists were ready.

"We'd better do it!" Dr. Sterling said. "The power's ready. Are you?"

Wayne gave him a thumbs-up signal. They both signaled to Diane.

"Look at Daddy, Adam," Diane said.

"Dada?"

"There he is. Daddy's going to take our picture. Smile for Dada. . . ."

Adam crinkled his forehead, trying to see his father. He was so small.

"Come on, Wayne," Diane said. "Say cheese, Adam."

Wayne flipped the switch.

"Cheese."

Zzzzzzzaaaaaaaappppp!

CHAPTER 20

"Oh, Adam!" Wayne said. Then he leaned down and picked up his very normal-size two-year-old son from the ground. Right after that, he gave his normal-size wife a hug. She took Adam from him and hugged him some more.

"You gave us quite a scare, little man," Dr. Sterling said, tickling Adam. Adam giggled. But he stayed the same size.

"I knew you could do it," Diane whispered in Wayne's ear. Those were the words he most needed to hear.

Then Dr. Hendrickson sauntered up to Wayne. "Well, Szalinski, you pulled it off. Who would have thought it possible?"

Diane had a few things she wanted to say to Dr. Hendrickson. "Dr. Hendrickson, that looked like a rifle of some sort that you were pointing at my baby."

"They were tranquilizer cartridges," he said. "They wouldn't have hurt him, I assure you."

Assurances from Dr. Hendrickson didn't mean anything to Diane. Adam didn't like them, either. He held his nose to show just how he felt about the man who had tried to shoot at him. Diane casually handed Adam to Wayne and then did what she'd been wanting to do for some time. She took a roundhouse swing and punched Dr. Hendrickson right in the nose! The scientist fell flat on his back. He was out like a light.

Adam cringed, "Ow-wee!"

"Never cross Mommy," Wayne advised his son.

Dr. Sterling waved to some of the medics who were standing by. "Could we have some help over here? Dr. Hendrickson has been overcome with excitement at the prospect of finding a new career. . . ."

Everything seemed so wonderful. Then Diane had a thought. It wasn't so wonderful.

"Wayne, the kids—Nick and Mandy!"

"Weren't they—oh no!—in Adam's pocket?"

"Don't tell me!" said Diane.

But Wayne told her. He had to. "Honey, I shrunk the kids!"

Wayne knew just what to do, because he'd done it before. The last time he'd shrunk the kids, he'd made himself some special equipment so he could find them. He instructed the police on what to bring from his house.

". . . And bring the dog, too!" he said.

*　　*　　*

In the cool desert night, Nick and Mandy sat next to each other in the front seat of the convertible, where they had landed when they fell out of Adam's pocket. On the car radio, a newscaster was giving a full report of what had gone on. Nick and Mandy had lived through it. They didn't need to listen to it.

"I guess your father's about the most famous guy in the world tonight," Mandy said. Now that the two of them weren't bouncing around in Adam's pocket, Mandy wasn't afraid anymore. In fact, she didn't seem to be afraid of *any*thing. She cuddled right up next to Nick. "And I guess you're about the bravest."

He blushed.

"Oh, it wasn't so much."

"How long do you think it will take before they find us?" Mandy asked.

"I don't know," he said. He hoped it would be a long, long time. Then he spotted something in the rearview mirror. It appeared to be a very big eye, magnified by a lens in front of it. It was a familiar eye, too. It was his father's eye.

"You're kind of, uh, different, Nick," Mandy said. "Like your dad."

"Oh, we're not that different," he said. He put his arm around Mandy. She snuggled up to him. The eye pulled back from the car.

"I guess the world needs people who are 'different,'" Mandy said. "It needs people who look at things, well, differently, I guess you could say." That made Nick feel very good.

"You found them?" Diane asked Wayne.

Wayne nodded. "But let's give them a few minutes," he said.

Diane was suspicious. "What's going on?" she demanded.

Wayne winked at Adam.

Adam peered into the little car sitting in the desert. Then held his nose.

Quark barked.

It was a perfectly normal day for the Szalinskis.

About the Author

B. B. Hiller is the author of more than fifty books for young readers, including the novelizations of *Honey, I Shrunk the Kids* and both Teenage Mutant Ninja Turtles movies. She lives in New York City with her two children, two cats, and a parakeet.